Happy Little Family

OTHER YEARLING BOOKS YOU WILL ENJOY:

SCHOOLHOUSE IN THE WOODS, Rebecca Caudill
UP AND DOWN THE RIVER, Rebecca Caudill
SCHOOLROOM IN THE PARLOR, Rebecca Caudill
SATURDAY COUSINS, Rebecca Caudill
ALL-OF-A-KIND FAMILY, Sydney Taylor
ALL-OF-A-KIND FAMILY UPTOWN, Sydney Taylor
ALL-OF-A-KIND FAMILY DOWNTOWN, Sydney Taylor
MORE ALL-OF-A-KIND FAMILY, Sydney Taylor
ELLA OF ALL-OF-A-KIND FAMILY, Sydney Taylor
THE VELVET ROOM, Zilpha Keatley Snyder

YEARLING BOOKS/YOUNG YEARLINGS/YEARLING CLASSICS are designed especially to entertain and enlighten young people. Patricia Reilly Giff, consultant to this series, received the bachelor's degree from Marymount College. She holds the master's degree in history from St. John's University, and a Professional Diploma in Reading from Hofstra University. She was a teacher and reading consultant for many years, and is the author of numerous books for young readers.

For a complete listing of all Yearling titles, write to
Dell Readers Service, P.O. Box 1045,
South Holland, IL 60473.

HAPPY LITTLE FAMILY

By

REBECCA CAUDILL

Illustrated by Decie Merwin

A Yearling Book

Published by
Dell Publishing
a division of
Bantam Doubleday Dell Publishing Group, Inc.
666 Fifth Avenue
New York, New York 10103

The author is indebted to *Trails*, a magazine for boys and girls published by the Methodist Publishing House, and to *Child Life*, published by The Open Road Publishing Company, for permission to include in this book some of the stories which appeared in those magazines.

Copyright © 1947 by Holt Rinehart and Winston
Copyright renewed © 1975 by Rebecca Caudill Ayars

All rights reserved. No part of this book may be reproduced or transmitted in any form or by any means, electronic or mechanical, including photocopying, recording, or by any information storage and retrieval system, without the written permission of the Publisher, except where permitted by law. For information address Henry Holt and Company, Inc., New York, New York.

The trademark Yearling® is registered in the U.S. Patent and Trademark Office.

ISBN: 0-440-40164-X

Reprinted by arrangement with Henry Holt and Company, Inc.

Printed in the United States of America

May 1989

10 9 8 7 6 5 4 3 2

CW

*This book
is especially for*
Becky Jean

Contents

	Page
Crack-the-Whip · · · · · · · · ·	1
The Pink Sunbonnet · · · · · · ·	22
The Arrowhead · · · · · · · · ·	42
The Red Toboggan Cap · · · · · ·	70
The Journey · · · · · · · · · ·	91

Happy Little Family

Crack-the-Whip

IT WAS January, and the morning was very cold. Icicles hung from the porch roof in a stiff ruffle. Sparrows sat hunched in the bare branches of the cherry tree, saying nothing. Only the wind made a noise. It howled down the mountain and whistled through the valley. It moaned in the pine trees and roared at the kitchen door. And everywhere it blew, it swept snowflakes before it and left them in deep white drifts.

That was outdoors. Indoors the morning was warm and cheery. A big fire burned in the fireplace of the log house and made a roaring noise up the chimney to scare the wind away.

Bonnie stood in front of the fire. First she stood facing the fire and held out her hands to warm them. Then she turned herself around and stood with her back to the fire, and held her hands behind her. Around and around she turned, warming herself.

At one side of the hearth stretched Rover, a yellow and white collie, fast asleep. He snored softly as he slept. The snoring made a cozy sound.

Curled up in Mother's hickory rocking chair lay Whiskers, a big black cat. As Bonnie turned herself the ninth time, Whiskers opened his eyes

a slit and looked at her. Then he shut them again and went on sleeping. He purred gently as he slept. The purring made a cozy sound.

Whenever her back was turned to the fire, Bonnie looked out the window. Beyond the road, along the edge of the mountains, wound the river. It was frozen solid, as it was always frozen in January, and people were sliding on the ice. Debby was there, and Emmy. Chris and Althy were there, and Father. Four of the Sawyers were there, three of the Huffs, and all five of the Watterson boys and girls. They made deep scars in the ice with their heavy hobnailed shoes as they slid back and forth, back and forth.

Bonnie blinked her eyes as she watched them. She could have been sliding on the ice too, instead of warming herself by the fire if only Debby and Emmy, Chris and Althy hadn't given her grown-up advice as they buttoned their coats and pulled on their warm mittens.

"Oh, Bonnie, sugar, you can't go," said Debby

when she saw Bonnie going for her coat. Debby
was six. She was pulling her bright red toboggan
cap low over her ears all the while she was
talking. "You're too little, Bonnie," said Debby.
"You were four only the day before yesterday."

"You'd freeze your toes right off, honey,"
Emmy told her.

Emmy was Bonnie's favorite sister. Emmy was eight, and twice as big as Bonnie. She could climb to the top of the sycamore tree in the barn lot. She could catch a ball with one hand as easily as Chris, who was ten, and she wasn't afraid of the dark, like Debby. Sometimes Emmy shared her treasures with Bonnie, half and half — the chestnuts she found on her way home from school, her snail shells, the rag dolls she made. But sliding on the ice was a thing Emmy wouldn't share.

"Shucks, Bonnie, you've got no idea how cold it is out there!" warned Chris.

"You'd just get in the way," said Althy. Althy was twelve.

Even Father, who always walked hand in hand with Bonnie when they went to the mountains looking for wintergreen or sweet wild straw-berries, seemed to understand no better than the others that she was now four, and big enough to go sliding on the ice.

Father, pulling on big brown mittens, smiled down at Bonnie and said nothing at all.

So Bonnie stayed home by the fire, warming herself. All the while she listened wistfully to the merry shouting that came from the river and did not once notice how softly Rover snored as he slept, nor how gently Whiskers purred as he lay curled up in Mother's rocking chair.

As Bonnie turned herself the tenth time, Mother came in from the kitchen.

"Br-r-r-r-r-r!" said Mother, making a noise like the wind. She held her hands out to the fire to warm them. "It must be cold out there on the river," she said.

"Emmy won't freeze her toes off, will she?" asked Bonnie.

"Oh, no," said Mother. "Emmy runs too fast."

"Will Debby?" asked Bonnie.

"Oh, no," said Mother. "Debby runs faster than Emmy."

"I wouldn't freeze my toes if I went skating on the ice, either," said Bonnie. "Would I?"

"I don't believe you would," said Mother.

"May I go skating then, Mother?" begged Bonnie. "I'm big enough. I'm four now."

Mother put her hand under Bonnie's chin. She tilted Bonnie's round face up and looked at it.

"Why, bless me, Bonnie!" she said. "You *are* four. I hadn't realized what a big girl you are. Run and get your coat."

Bonnie trotted to the kitchen, her copper-toed shoes thudding softly across the bright rag carpet of the living room, clicking across the bare floor of the kitchen.

Hammered into the wall behind the kitchen stove, in a pattern like stair steps, were five nails. The farthest one belonged to Althy, because she was the oldest and could reach the highest. The next one belonged to Chris. The one in the middle belonged to Emmy. The next to the lowest nail belonged to Debby. The lowest of all was Bonnie's.

All the nails were empty except Bonnie's. On her nail hung a blue worsted coat made from an old coat of Father's, and a pair of new mittens, as red as ripe cherries. After Mother had knitted the mittens, she made a special loop on them to hang them by.

Bonnie stood looking at the nails. She might as well try to reach the kitchen ceiling, or the stove pipe, as Althy's nail, she thought. Althy's nail was very high. Chris's nail was high too, and Emmy's. She moved a step farther behind the stove and stood in front of Debby's nail. Being four the day before yesterday, and going on five, she thought she might be able to reach Debby's nail.

She raised herself on the copper toes of her shoes. She stretched as far as her finger tips could reach on the wall. She grunted, and that helped her stretch farther still. But she could not quite reach Debby's nail.

"I'm getting bigger now, and soon I can reach it," she said to herself.

"I'll tie my fascinator around your head to keep your ears warm," Mother told her when she brought her coat and mittens from the kitchen.

"When may I have a toboggan cap, Mother?" asked Bonnie. "A red toboggan, like Debby's, with a white tassel?"

"When you're bigger I'll knit you one," promised Mother.

Crossing the ends of the big blue fascinator under Bonnie's chin, Mother tied them in a bow in the back. "Run along, now," she said.

At the edge of the river Bonnie stopped to watch the others sliding. They were running races on the ice and playing tag. They were whizzing along as fast as the wind. They were laughing and shouting to one another — Althy and Chris, Emmy and Debby, the four Sawyers, the three Huffs, the five Wattersons and Father.

Far up the river Bonnie saw Debby in her red coat. Debby took a long run on the ice, planted her feet firmly, one a little in front of the other, spread her arms wide and skimmed along like a red autumn leaf flying in the wind.

Out on the ice walked Bonnie. Being four, and going on five, she was sure she could skate as well as Debby. She took one step. Two steps. Half a dozen steps. Then she planted her feet just as she had seen Debby do, one a little in front of the other. Nothing happened at all.

Once more she watched as Debby came skimming along on the ice. Once more she tried. Three steps. Four steps. Five steps. Not quite running steps like Debby's, but hurrying steps, in between running and walking. Six steps. Seven steps. Then a push to set herself going.

Plop! Both feet flew from under her. Both copper toes shot into the air.

Bonnie lay very still a moment, wanting to cry; but four was too big for crying, she decided. So she got to her feet again on the slippery ice, and looked once more for Debby.

Down, down the river came Debby, her arms spread wide.

"Debby!" called Bonnie.

"Hi there, Bonnie!" shouted Debby, waving to her. "Watch me skate, Bonnie! Did Mother say you could come?"

Without waiting for an answer, Debby took another run-and-go, and slid away, down the river.

Bonnie blinked her eyes after Debby. Father had said Debby was such a good skater he thought he ought to buy a pair of metal skates for her like a pair he had once seen in the town across the mountains. Then Debby could whiz by so fast she wouldn't look like a girl. She would look like a bright red bird flying down the river. Father was proud of Debby's skating.

Remembering the skates Father was going to bring to Debby, Bonnie felt almost as small as three, which, when one is four, is very small.

"Never mind," she said to herself. "I'll find Emmy. Emmy will help me."

13

Down the river came Emmy. Emmy was sliding even faster than Debby, but she fell down twice.

"Emmy!"called Bonnie.

At the sound of Bonnie's voice, Emmy swung about. She ran over to Bonnie, her eyes shining.

"Oh, Bonnie!" she laughed. "Don't you look sweet, all tied up in Mother's fascinator! Did Mother say you could come, honey? Watch me skate!"

And Emmy was off down the river after Debby.

Bonnie looked for Althy. Althy was doing fancy stunts on the ice. She glided along with her hands behind her. Then, with her hands over her head, she slid along first on one foot, then on the other. Althy was proud of her skating.

"Oh, Althy!" Bonnie called.

Althy put both feet on the ice and came to a stop.

"Bonnie!" she said. Her voice sounded grown up and scolding. "You'd better run back to the house before you freeze. Did Mother say you could come?"

Without another word, Althy lifted one foot and slid away on the other.

A lump that felt like a cry lump stuck in Bonnie's throat. Maybe Chris would hold her hand, she thought, until she could get her feet going on the ice. Chris was racing with Andy Watterson. They were running on the ice, whizzing around curves, cutting sharp corners.

"Chris, will you help me?" Bonnie called, when he came close enough to hear.

Chris, flying along with Andy at his coattail, shouted, "Look out there, Bonnie! Better get out of the way! Hey, did Mother say you could come?"

At last Father spied Bonnie. He slid across the river straight to her.

"How did you get here, Bonnie?" he asked,

smiling down at her. But he didn't stop for an answer. "Wait a minute," he said, "until I come back."

Before Andy Watterson could catch Chris, or Althy could twirl on her toes twelve times, Father came back. On one arm he carried Mother's three-legged kitchen chair. On the other arm was a warm red blanket.

"That for me?" called Bonnie.

"It's for you," said Father. "You're going skating."

Father unfolded the blanket. He spread it
on the chair and lifted Bonnie into it. Then
he wrapped her up snugly until all that showed
of her were her blue eyes and her small red
nose.

"Ready?" asked Father. "Here we go!"

Pushing the chair in front of him, Father slid
out to the middle of the river.

"Look at Bonnie!" shouted Debby, who
whizzed by just then. Quickly she wheeled

about, caught one of Father's hands, and skated along with him.

"Look at Bonnie!" cried Emmy. She caught Debby's hand.

Althy glided to them on one foot, and took Emmy's hand.

"Hey! Let's play crack-the-whip!" shouted Chris. He took Althy's hand. "Come on, Andy! Come on, everybody! Let's play crack-the-whip!"

Down the river they glided — Father and

Debby and Emmy, Althy and Chris, the four Sawyers, the three Huffs and the five Wattersons. Flying over the ice, at the head of the line, sat Bonnie in Mother's kitchen chair, her eyes dancing, her small nose growing redder and redder every minute in the wind.

Up the river and down they went. Up the river and down.

At every turn Father pulled hard on Debby's hand, and the long line went flying wide like the lashing of a whip. Every time Father cracked the whip, Chris and Althy, one of the Huffs, half of the Sawyers and all five of the Wattersons fell sprawling on the ice.

"Like it, Bonnie?" asked Father.

Bonnie was too muffled up to make a sound, but she nodded her head and wiggled the blanket with her feet to tell Father it was the most fun she had had since the day before yesterday, when she was four.

Then, suddenly, she didn't like it any more.

Only little girls, girls of two and three, were pushed about in kitchen chairs over the ice, she remembered. Big girls like Debby skimmed away on their own feet. She decided she wouldn't ride in a chair again. Riding in a chair, she would never grow as big as Debby.

The Pink Sunbonnet

ONE MORNING in spring, after the ice on the river had melted and the warm sun had driven winter north over the mountains, Father put Mother's sidesaddle on little brown Mag. Mother mounted Mag and rode across the river to the store. She came home bringing many bundles.

Althy and Chris, Emmy and Debby, and Bonnie crowded around her.

"Here's something for you, Althy," said Mother. She handed Althy a brown paper package, short and flat, and tied with a white string.

Althy untied the string, unfolded the paper, and lifted out some flower-sprinkled dimity cloth. Out of the cloth rolled a spool of white thread.

"Oh, Mother, how pretty!" said Althy. "Will you help me cut out a dress this afternoon? I want to wear it Sunday."

Mother handed Chris two packages. They were both thin, one thinner than the other.

Chris opened the package that was not so thin, and found inside a necktie just like Father's. He had never had a necktie before.

"Look, Father!" he said. "I'm almost as big as you are now." He held up the necktie proudly for everyone to see. "Thank you, Mother," he said.

"You have another package too," Mother reminded him.

The other package was no bigger than a pencil. The paper was twisted at both ends.

Chris untwisted the paper and out dangled a pair of shoestrings.

At once Chris sat down on the floor and began to take the old strings out of his shoes. He had broken them so many times and had knotted them so many times in odd places to make them last through the winter that lately he hadn't bothered to tie them at all.

"Don't jerk so hard on these new strings when you lace them, Chris," Mother told him. "Then you won't break them so quickly. You'll be going barefoot soon. These new strings ought to last until then."

While Mother was giving Chris this good advice, Chris was threading a string in one of his shoes. He laced it to the top and tied it in a bowknot. Then he looked at it. He laced the other shoe and tied the string in a bow-

knot. He stuck his feet straight in front of him and everyone admired the new shoestrings.

"You don't look like the same brother we've had around all winter," Emmy told him.

"I don't feel the same, either," said Chris. "New shoestrings make you feel new inside. Thank you, Mother," he said.

Mother handed Emmy a big white box tied with green string. "Here's something for you and Debby, Emmy," she said.

All of them crowded closer, because the box, being big, must have in it something even more special than flower-sprinkled cloth for a new dress, or a necktie like Father's, or new shoe-strings. Emmy picked at the hard, tight knot in the string. Debby grew impatient, yanked at the string and broke it.

Emmy lifted the lid. Debby snatched off the white paper that lay on top.

"Oh!" cried Debby.

"Oh!" sighed Emmy. "New hats!"

In the box were two hats, made of straw. The wide brims were turned up all around. A broad white ribbon circled each crown and fell in long white streamers down the back. On the front of one hat was a bunch of blue forget-me-nots. On the front of the other was a bunch of pink forget-me-nots.

"The pink one is for you, Emmy," said Mother. "It matches your cheeks. The blue one is yours, Debby. It matches your eyes."

"Thank you, Mother," said Debby and Emmy.

Bonnie took a step nearer the box and peeped in. She thought Mother might have brought her a hat too. Now that she was four, she thought surely she was big enough to have a straw hat with white streamers down the back and white forget-me-nots the color of her hair in front. But there was nothing more in the box.

Debby and Emmy put their hats on and went

to stand in front of the mirror. Soon they began to argue.

"Mine's prettier than yours, Emmy," said
Debby.

"It isn't, either," said Emmy. "Pink is always
prettier than blue."

"Mine *is* prettier!" declared Debby. "And
look! My streamers are lots longer than yours.
Mine come down to my waist."

"That's because you're not nearly so tall as
I am," Emmy told her.

All the while they were arguing, Bonnie stood looking at their fine, new hats, wishing and wishing that she might have one too. If she had a big straw hat with long white streamers down the back and white forget-me-nots in the front of it, she would be so proud she couldn't think of any words for arguing.

"And this is for you, Bonnie," Mother said.

Bonnie turned and looked. Mother handed her the last package, a small, flat one.

"Thank you, Mother," said Bonnie.

She began fumbling with the string. She was in a great hurry, for she thought that maybe — just maybe — a hat was inside the brown wrapping paper. Of course, the package wasn't shaped like a hat. It didn't feel like a hat. Still, she told herself, a person can never tell about hats.

"Let me help you untie the string, Bonnie," said Father.

Bonnie ran to Father with the package. He

opened his jackknife and cut the string. Bonnie laid back the brown wrapping paper. Inside lay some pink gingham cloth.

"I'm going to make you a new sunbonnet," said Mother.

A sunbonnet! Last year when she was only three, Bonnie had had a sunbonnet. A blue one. She didn't want another sunbonnet. She wanted a hat — a big straw hat with long white streamers down the back and a bunch of white forget-me-nots in front. A hat like Debby's

and Emmy's. She wanted a hat more than any-thing else in the world.

Bonnie's chin began to quiver. Tears swam about in her eyes.

"Never mind, Bonnie," said Father, "I wouldn't cry. Sunbonnets are better than hats. You wait and see."

Just then Rover set up a loud barking in the barn lot.

"Hadn't we better go and see what Rover is barking about?" said Father.

They set out for the barn lot, hand in hand, and found Rover barking at Whiskers, who was spitting at him from the limb of a sycamore tree. Bonnie almost forgot the hats.

The next day Mother made Bonnie's sunbon-net. First she took the scissors and cut *snip, snip, snip* through the pink cloth. Then she opened up the sewing machine. With her feet she pumped the treadle. With her hands she held the cloth. Up and down flew the needle.

Around and around whirled the wheel. *Jerk, jerk* went the spool of thread as the pink cloth ate it up.

Back of the sewing machine stood Bonnie, watching the bonnet grow. It was going to have long streamers on each side to tie in a bow under her chin. It was going to have a ruffle all around the edge. Bonnie held her hands back of the needle and caught the ruffle as it came through. Mother treadled so fast

she made the machine jiggle. Bonnie's hands jiggled too.

Only once did Bonnie leave the sewing machine. Once she tiptoed to the closet where Debby and Emmy kept their new hats. She lifted the box lid and peeped in. Debby's hat with the blue forget-me-nots lay on top.

Cautiously Bonnie lifted Debby's hat out of the box and put it on her head. She stood on a chair in front of the mirror and then looked at

herself. The streamers that came down to Debby's waist fell almost to her knees. They were exactly the right length for a girl her size, she thought.

A door opened.

Bonnie jerked the hat off her head and ran to the closet with it. She put it back in the box quickly, and pushed the lid on, tight. Then she hurried back to the sewing machine to watch the sunbonnet grow.

Through the house came Debby, making straight for the closet door. She went to the hatbox and lifted the lid.

"Mother!" she called. Her voice sounded dangerous — quite, quite dangerous. "Bonnie's been trying on my hat," she said. "She's put it back in the box upside down."

Debby came into the room where Mother was making the sunbonnet and caught sight of Bonnie, who by this time was standing behind the sewing machine.

"Bonnie!" she scolded. "You did have on my hat, didn't you?"

"Yes," said Bonnie.

"Well, you let it alone. Don't take it out of that box again. It isn't yours. It's mine."

"Oh, Debby!" said Mother, in a shocked voice. "A new hat will never make you pretty. Pretty is as pretty does." Mother said that to Debby a dozen times a day: "Pretty is as pretty does."

"A new hat is a lot of bother, isn't it, Bonnie?" Mother said, turning back to the sewing machine. "I believe a sunbonnet like yours is best."

The next day Aunt Cassie, who lived across the river, sent word for Emmy and Debby and Bonnie to come and spend the afternoon with her. Sometimes they waded across the river where the water was shallow. That afternoon, however, Father was going to the store, and he took them across the river on Mag.

Bonnie rode on the pommel of the saddle in

front of Father. She wore her new pink sunbonnet. If she looked up, she could see the sun shining through the narrow ruffle. If she looked down, she could see the big bow tied neatly under her chin. It was as pretty a sunbonnet as she had ever seen, but it was not like a hat.

Debby sat behind Father on Mag and held onto Father's waist. She wore her new straw hat with the long white streamers in the back and the blue forget-me-nots in front.

Emmy sat behind Debby and held onto Debby's waist. She wore her new hat with the long white streamers in the back and the pink forget-me-nots in front.

Away down the road jogged Mag, bouncing Debby and Emmy up and down when she trotted. When she came to the shallow river crossing, she stepped down off the bank into the water with a great splash. Her back was like a steep hill.

"Debby, your hat's right in my eye," complained Emmy. "Can't you hold your head to one side a little?"

"I can't hold it to one side any more than I am already," Debby told her. "You sit back a little."

"But I can't sit back," said Emmy. "I'm almost sitting on the horse's tail now. Ouch! You hit me square in the eye just then!"

"Well, sit back!" Debby said.

"I can't!"

"Well, don't blame it on my hat," said Debby.

By this time Mag was halfway across the river. Suddenly she stumbled on a rock, causing Debby's hat to strike Emmy in the face. The brim of Emmy's hat tangled with the streamers of Debby's hat. Emmy jerked backward and Debby jerked forward. Off tumbled both hats. Down, down they floated, straight into the river.

"Father!" screamed Emmy. "Our hats! Look what Debby did to our hats!"

"I didn't!" shouted Debby. "You did it, Emmy!"

Debby began to cry loudly.

Father turned in the saddle and looked. The hats were riding along over the ripples like little boats, their long white streamers trailing behind.

The hats didn't go far. Before long Debby's hat caught on a stone. Emmy's floated to safety on a limb sticking out of the water.

Father guided Mag to driftwood that lay ahead of them in the river.

"Get off on this driftwood, Emmy," Father said. "You and Debby. Take off your shoes and stockings and wade after your hats. We'll wait for you, Bonnie and I."

Bonnie watched them. They weren't speaking to each other as they pulled off their shoes and stockings. They weren't going to have a very good time at Aunt Cassie's, all on account of their hats.

"If I had a hat, I wouldn't let it fall in the river," said Bonnie.

"If I were a girl," said Father, "I believe I'd rather have a sunbonnet. At least, until I was big enough to wear a hat without quarreling about it."

Bonnie glanced up through the narrow pink ruffle of the sunbonnet and noticed that the sunlight shining through was as soft as candlelight. She glanced down at the streamers tied tightly in a big bow under her chin and was glad that they were dry, not dripping wet like the forlorn hat streamers.

"I just believe I'd rather have a sunbonnet," said Father.

"A pink sunbonnet like mine, Father?" Bonnie asked.

"As exactly like yours as I could make it," said Father.

40

Bonnie thought about this for a minute.

"But I do like hats," she said. "Don't you think I'm big enough to have a hat, Father?"

"Almost," said Father.

"When will I be big enough?" asked Bonnie.

"All too soon," said Father.

The Arrowhead

ONE SUMMER morning Father went to hoe the corn in the field in the river bend. When he came home at dinner time, he had an Indian arrowhead in his pocket.

Althy had a small arrowhead collection. When she was ten, she was very proud of her arrowheads of many colors and sizes. Now that she was twelve and spent much of her time braiding her light brown hair in front of the mirror, she had grown tired of arrowheads. With some of her collection she had paid Chris to dry the dishes for her. Some she had given to Debby, and some to Andy Watterson. She had kept only the prettiest ones.

Chris had so many arrowheads that he had lost count of them. He had one shoe box full, and another half full. Most of them he had picked up in the fields and on the mountains. A few of them Father had given to him, and some he had swapped with Andy Watterson. He had dark gray ones and light gray ones, and dark gray ones with light gray streaks in them. He had white arrowheads and black ones, pink ones and blue ones and greenish ones. And, besides, he had one Indian hammer, two Indian tomahawks, four Indian knives, one Indian spearhead, and one Indian hoe. The hammer and the tomahawks, the knives and the spearhead he kept in still another shoe box,

but the hoe was so large he laid it in a corner of his room.

Emmy had a middle-sized collection of arrowheads. The shoe box in which she kept them was half full.

Debby had a larger collection of arrowheads than Emmy. Debby was good at finding arrowheads when she went walking over the mountain to play with the Wattersons, or carrying water to Father when he was working in the fields. Debby had an arrowhead eye, Father said.

Bonnie had no arrowheads. Whenever she went with Debby across the plowed fields to carry water to Father, she kept her eyes fastened on the ground, looking for an arrowhead. But Debby always saw the arrowheads first.

"It's easy to see them when you're six, like me," said Debby.

"I'm almost six," said Bonnie. "I'm long past four."

"But you can't find arrowheads yet," said Debby.

With so many arrowheads in one family, it would seem there must be one of every size and shape and color. But the arrowhead Father found when he went to hoe the corn was not like any other arrowhead in the house. It was chipped of red flint, the color of the sky on a summer morning when it is going to rain. The edges were almost as sharp as the blade of Father's jackknife. On each side of the stem was a design like the petal of a dogwood flower.

Father washed the dirt from the arrowhead. Then he rubbed the flint with a cloth until it glowed like fire.

"What are you going to do with it, Father?" asked Althy. "May I have it, please? I want it for a keepsake."

Althy wanted the arrowhead to put in the gold jewel box she had been given at Christmas. She kept all her treasures in the gold

jewel box, and no one, not even Mother, knew where she hid the tiny gold key with which she locked the lid.

"Father, may I have it?" asked Chris. "I'm the one who is really interested in arrowheads. I ought to have it for my collection."

Emmy and Debby looked longingly at the arrowhead too. So did Bonnie. She wished Father would give it to her to start a collection.

But Father walked over to the fireplace and stood the arrowhead on the mantel.

"I'm going to give it to the one who earns it," he said. "The Indians were brave people and often very wise. The Indian who made this arrowhead was an artist too. I'll give it to the one who proves that he is as brave and as wise as the Indians were."

"But how can we prove that we are brave?" asked Chris. "And wise?" He wanted the arrowhead more than ever, now that it was on the mantel to be seen but not to be touched.

"By the way you use your head," said Father.

"But I do the same things every day," said Chris. "I feed the horse, and plow, and cut stovewood. Some days I go fishing. Some days I go to play with Andy Watterson. The same things happen every day. I use my head the same way every day. I don't see any chance to prove that I am either brave or wise." Chris couldn't understand Father at all.

"Some days are different," said Father. "Some day when you don't expect it, a chance to prove

47

you are brave and wise will be standing right in front of you."

"This day?" asked Debby. Debby was planning to go outdoors as soon as she finished drying the dinner dishes and begin to watch for a chance. She might have a chance eye, she thought, the way she had an arrowhead eye.

"Maybe," said Father. "Nobody knows. But you must look and listen sharply, or else the chance may slip by without your seeing it."

Because she was watching the hardest, Debby was the first to meet a chance to be brave. She met it in the evening when Mother sent her to the corncrib to bring nubbins for Pied the cow.

Pied was mooing at the barn-lot gate. She had a new calf lying in the stable, and she was anxious for Debby to open the gate and let her into the stable to see her calf.

Before bringing the nubbins from the corncrib, Debby went into the stable to pet the new calf. It wasn't pied like its mother. It was just

the color of Debby's hair, which once had been
white like Bonnie's but which had begun to
turn golden. Debby rubbed the calf's back. She
smoothed the white spot on its face. She patted
it on the head. She held her fingers in front of
it and let it lick them with its rough little
tongue. This she liked best of all.

Pied, mooing at the barn-lot gate, did not
like it at all. She was afraid Debby might hurt
the calf. She grew more anxious every minute.

Finally she lifted her front feet and jumped. Over the gate she sailed and made straight for the stable, her voice angry, her head low. She meant to butt Debby right up the stable wall. She would have done so, too, if Debby had not heard her coming.

As fast as a mouse scurrying from a cat, Debby scurried up the stable ladder to the hayloft. There she sat in the hay, panting from fright, while down below Pied licked her calf and mooed threateningly.

For a long time Debby sat in the hay, wondering what to do. If she stayed up there, she couldn't feed Pied her nubbins. If she came down for the nubbins, she had to pass by the cow and calf. Every time she started toward the ladder, Pied mooed more threateningly than before. At last Debby began to cry.

"Mother!" she called through her tears. "Mother, please come here!"

But Mother did not hear her.

She called Chris, who had gone to the pasture to pick blackberries. She called Althy, who was looking at herself in the mirror. She called Emmy, who was churning for Mother, and Bonnie, who was carrying in stovewood. No one heard her, neither Chris nor Althy, neither Emmy nor Bonnie.

Suddenly, sitting on the hay in the hayloft, Debby realized she had met a chance to be brave. She stopped crying. When she stopped crying, Pied stopped mooing at her.

Debby began to think of ways to make friends with Pied, for she knew that, as long as the cow was angry, she could never climb down the ladder and go past her to the corncrib. Maybe, she thought, if she carried down an armful of sweet-smelling hay and gave it to Pied, the cow might let her pass safely by.

Pied mooed softly as Debby climbed down the ladder. Her nose quivered as she smelled the hay.

"So-o-o, Pied!" said Debby. "So-o-o!"

Her voice was small with fear, and she had to scold her feet to keep them from running back up the ladder.

"So-o-o-o, Pied!" she said.

Slowly she came down, stopping on every rung. But she didn't go back. And she didn't call for help. When Pied stretched her neck, Debby held out the hay to her. With her long dark tongue the cow scooped up a mouthful of hay. Debby laid the rest of it in front of her. Then she went to the corncrib for the nubbins, very much pleased with herself.

When she came back, to make sure there was no mistake about her being brave, she held out a nubbin to Pied. The cow took it in her mouth. Debby wasn't scared at all, not even when Pied's big, rough tongue licked her fingers.

That night at supper time Debby told Father what had happened. "Was I brave enough to win the arrowhead, Father?" she asked.

"I'll study about it," said Father.

The next day, which was Wednesday, Father sent Chris across the mountain to ask Andy Watterson's father to help him cut hay on Thursday. It was the middle of the afternoon when Chris started. He walked down the road whistling. Chris whistled everywhere he went. Father said he was the whistlingest boy in all the mountains.

"You'd better go along fast," Mother called after him, "or else dark will catch you before you get home."

Chris went fast enough. But when he had given Mr. Watterson Father's message, he stayed to tell Andy about the red arrowhead that Father had found. Then Andy showed him a new arrowhead he had found. Then Chris wanted to see all of Andy's collection again, just in case Andy might have an arrowhead as red as Father's. At last, when Chris remembered to start home, it was after sundown.

Exactly on top of the mountain, dark caught him.

Being still a long way from home, Chris stopped whistling and started to run. But to run down a mountain through dark woods at night is to head straight into trouble.

Soon the path turned, but Chris kept running in the direction he had started. He landed in a thorn tree and had to pick himself out and find his way back to the path. Three times he stumped his toes on the roots of trees. At last he decided that a dark mountain path was no place to hurry; so he began to walk.

As he walked, he heard big noises. Once he was sure he heard a wildcat spring from a limb to the ground, but it was only a haw dropping from a tree — a little red haw the size of the end of his thumb. Another time he thought he heard a shotgun, and he wondered if the Indians had come back to hunt in the mountains, but it was only a dead twig snapping.

Suddenly, in the branches of an oak tree directly over him he heard the biggest noise of all.

"Whoo-oo-oo-oo!"

Chris remembered stories of Indians who signaled to each other by whoo-oo-oo-ooing like owls. A little trickle of fear ran all the way from the top of his head down to his feet, and he froze in his tracks. Then he began to run, as if for his life, down the steep mountain path. Before he had taken six steps, a tree root tripped him, and he sprawled headlong on the ground. He fell so hard that he knocked the breath out of himself, and he couldn't get up right away.

Lying in the path, he realized a chance to be brave was waiting for him there on the dark mountain.

Slowly he got to his feet. Slowly he started down the path once more.

"Didn't you ever hear an owl before?" he said to himself, scoldingly. "Just a little old screech owl that never hurt a thing but mice?"

The rest of the way down the mountain, he walked. At first he whistled to show he was not afraid, but before he reached the foot of the mountain he stopped whistling. It would be too bad to have anyone mistake his bravery, he told himself, because of whistling a little tune.

At home he told Father what had happened. "Was I brave enough to win the arrowhead, Father?" he asked.

"I'll think it over," said Father thoughtfully.

The next day Debby and Emmy were in the back yard jumping over an old wooden box. They gave each other three trials, first Emmy, then Debby.

They started at the woodshed, which was quite a distance from the box, ran with all their might, and jumped. On the second trial, they started at the clothesline pole, which was only half as far. When they jumped, their pig-

tails flew out behind them. Emmy's pigtails looked like golden ropes, for her hair was much longer than Debby's, and a shade more golden.

At last Emmy was ready to jump over the box flat-footed. She stood directly in front of it, placed her feet together, flapped her arms like wings, jumped, and crash-landed in a corner of the box. A rusty nail caught her at the ankle and scraped her leg to her knee. Blood trickled down her leg.

Mother heard the crash and came hurrying to the kitchen door. She took one look at Emmy's leg and one look at the rusty nail.

"We'll have to wash that cut with turpentine," she said.

"No!" screamed Emmy.

Emmy knew all about turpentine. She knew how it smarted and stung and burned when it was scrubbed into a cut.

"No! No!" she screamed again. The tears flowed out of her blue eyes in two little streams.

"Sit down here," said Mother, half pushing Emmy into the three-legged kitchen chair while she went for the turpentine and a clean white cloth. Debby and Bonnie stood watching Emmy sorrowfully. They knew all about turpentine too.

"When I begin to wash out the cut, instead of crying, Emmy, just yell 'Oops!' " said Mother.

"I can't! I can't!" cried Emmy, holding her leg. She was shaking her head, and her long golden pigtails were swinging from side to side.

"Why, you're my bravest girl, Emmy," said Mother. "Surely you aren't going to cry about a thing like turpentine!"

Then, suddenly, Emmy saw waiting there in the kitchen a chance to be brave. She stopped crying. She gritted her teeth hard. She held onto the chair. She squeezed her blue eyes shut, and waited. When the turpentine burned, she yelled "Oops!" When it burned like fire, she yelled "Oops! Oops! *Oops!*" Before Mother finished washing the cut, Emmy stopped saying

"Oops!" She said nothing at all, so that there might be no mistake about her bravery. She didn't even wiggle.

When Father came home to dinner Emmy told him about the rusty nail and the turpentine bath. "Was I brave enough to earn the arrowhead, Father?" she asked.

"I'll see," said Father.

A week later, at sundown, Mother called Althy to go to the pasture for Pied. Althy was in front of the mirror, tying a pink ribbon at the top and another pink ribbon at the bottom of the long light brown braid that hung down her back.

"Want to come, Bonnie?" Althy asked, taking a last look at herself.

Bonnie went running. She liked going to the pasture for Pied. She especially liked going with Althy. Althy knew where to find wintergreen leaves to chew as they walked along, and May apples, and buckeyes to put in their pockets,

and puff balls to burst with their feet. She knew stories to tell to Bonnie, and guessing games to play with her as they walked along.

They walked to the top of the hill where they let down the bars. They went through the woods, and across the pasture, calling: "Sukey! Sukey! Sukey!"

High in the hilly pasture, Pied was eating clover. When she saw Althy and Bonnie, she set out for home, her bell tinkling a silver tune

as she hurried to see her calf. Behind her
walked Bonnie, always a little ahead of Althy,
back across the pasture, and through the still,
dim woods.

Bonnie had almost reached the bars.

"Bonnie!" Althy called to her. "Stand still
where you are. Stand very still and don't
move."

Bonnie stood very still and didn't move.
Althy had thought up a new game to play with
her, she thought.

"Turn around now," commanded Althy.
"Toward me."

Bonnie turned toward Althy.

"Now walk to me," said Althy. "Slowly.
Don't run. Don't run a step!"

Bonnie plodded along as slowly as a tortoise.
When finally she reached Althy, Althy stooped
and put her arms about her and held her safely.

"Look, Bonnie!" she said, pointing toward
the bars.

There in the path, beside the bars, lay a rattlesnake, coiled round and round, ready to strike, its rattles sizzling with anger.

"Will it hurt us?" whimpered Bonnie, putting her arms tightly about Althy's neck.

"Not now," said Althy.

"What shall we do?" asked Bonnie. She felt like crying, but when she saw that Althy was not crying, she decided not to cry, either. It made her feel quite big.

"We'll just wait until it decides to go away," said Althy.

They waited and watched. In a short time the rattlesnake felt good-humored again. The rattles on the end of its tail quieted down. It uncoiled itself and slithered away from the path through the dead leaves. Althy, holding Bonnie's hand tightly in her own, hurried through the bars and down the hill.

That night at the supper table Althy told Father what had happened.

"How far was Bonnie from the snake?" asked Father, his face very serious.

"Only one step," said Althy. "One little step, the size of Bonnie's."

"How did you happen to see the snake?" asked Father.

"I heard it first," said Althy. "I heard it shaking its rattles, and I knew it was somewhere close."

"Ugh!" said Debby. "Didn't you scream, Althy? I'd have screamed."

"If I had screamed, I would have scared Bonnie, and she might have stepped on the snake," said Althy.

"Why didn't you run?" asked Emmy. "I think I would have run."

"Why did you tell Bonnie to walk?" Chris asked. "I would have told her to grease her heels and fly."

"If Bonnie had run, she might have made the snake much madder than it already was," explained Althy. "And then it might have struck her."

Father's face was still serious as he got up from the table. He walked straight to the mantel, took down the Indian arrowhead and handed it to Althy.

"You are as brave as any Indian ever was, Althy," he said, "and wiser than most of them. You have won the arrowhead."

"I think Althy deserves it too," said Mother.

Chris and Emmy, Debby and Bonnie looked once more at the red arrowhead, with the dogwood petals carved on the stem of it, as Althy laid it away in her gold jewel box and locked the lid.

After a moment, Chris spoke. "I think Bonnie ought to have an arrowhead too," he said. "She didn't cry. She didn't run. She did just what Althy told her to. Remember that greenish one of mine, Bonnie, with the white band across it? I think I'll give you that one."

He ran up the stairs to his room, and came back with the arrowhead.

"Thank you, Chris," said Bonnie.

Debby gave her an arrowhead, too, and Emmy gave her three arrowheads.

"Now I can start a collection," said Bonnie. "Like Debby's."

"Until you're big enough to find arrowheads yourself, you can't make a real collection," Debby reminded her.

"I'll start looking in the morning," said Bonnie. "I think I'll be big enough in the morning."

"It's bedtime now, Bonnie," said Mother. "I'll help you wash your feet tonight."

"I'll help you undress, Bonnie," said Father, when Mother finished drying her feet.

Hand in hand, Bonnie and Father went up the stairs to the room where she slept with Emmy. While Bonnie talked about arrowheads, Father unbuttoned her dress for her, buttoned her nightie, and hung her clothes on a chair. He heard her say her "Now I lay me down to sleep," lifted her into bed, pulled the cover up to her chin, and kissed her good night.

The Red Toboggan Cap

ONE SATURDAY morning in the late fall, Chris and Emmy, Debby and Bonnie were on their way across the mountain to play with the Watterson children. Andy Watterson had a new puppy. He wanted them to see it.

Father was already at the Wattersons'. He had gone at daybreak to help Andy's father chop down trees on the mountain side.

A chilly wind was rustling among the trees on the mountain, scattering before it red sumac leaves, and golden poplar leaves, and brown leaves from the oak trees.

"Bet it's going to snow soon," said Chris, as they were getting ready to go.

"Bet the geese had better fly south soon," said Emmy.

"Bet the squirrels had better store away lots of nuts," said Debby. "Bet the bears had better get to bed for the winter."

"Bet I'd better wear my new toboggan cap,"
spoke up Bonnie.

The week before Mother had knitted the cap.
It was long and red, like Debby's, with a white
tassel at the end. It was soft as a kitten and warm
as feathers. It was hanging on Bonnie's nail behind the kitchen stove, waiting for the first
frosty day. To see it hanging beside Debby's
made Bonnie feel that, at last, she was surely
growing big.

"Yes, Bonnie, today you may wear your new

toboggan," said Mother. "All of you must wrap up warmly. It will be cold crossing the mountain."

Up the mountain path they climbed, Chris in front, whistling, Debby next, then Bonnie, and Emmy. Up and up and up they climbed until they reached the spot where the owl whoo-oo-oo-ooed at Chris when he stayed too late at Andy Watterson's and dark caught him on the mountain. The log house and the stable, the road and the river were far below them.

In spite of the fact that they wanted to see Andy's new puppy, they didn't go very fast. Emmy and Chris threw stones at trees to see who could hit nearest the middle of the trunks. Debby stopped now and then to collect acorn cups to use for dishes in her playhouse. Bonnie stopped because the others stopped.

The path they were following forked on top of the mountain. One path led by a round-about way down to the Wattersons' house in the

valley. The other path followed for a distance along the top of the mountain, then dropped directly down to the house.

"Which way shall we go this morning?" asked Chris when they reached the fork in the path. "The roundabout way is longer, but it isn't so steep."

"Let's go the roundabout way," suggested Debby. "I know where a burr oak tree is. It has big shaggy acorn cups that I can use for bowls."

"Let's go down the steep way," said Bonnie.

"Oh, let's not, Bonnie," Debby told her. She started at once down the roundabout path. "Come on, everybody," she said. "I'm going this way."

Chris started following after Debby. Emmy took Bonnie's hand and started too.

Bonnie wouldn't follow. "I'm going the steep way," she said.

"Oh, you can't, Bonnie," Emmy told her. "You must come with us."

"I can go the steep way alone," said Bonnie. "I can find the way. I'm big enough."

"What makes you want to go alone, Bonnie?" asked Chris. All of them had to stop until the argument was settled.

"It's because she has that new red toboggan cap," explained Debby. "She feels grown up because she has a toboggan like mine."

"I am grown up," announced Bonnie. "I'll soon be five."

"But even grown-up people don't go down the mountain alone when there is somebody to go with them," explained Emmy. "Do you want me to go with you?"

"No," answered Bonnie. "I want to go alone."

"She's being stubborn," said Debby. "That's different from being grown up."

"You went this way by yourself one time," Bonnie said to Debby. "And I'm as big as you are."

"Oh, all right," said Chris. "We'll never get to Andy's house this way." He was growing impatient. "You're not so big as Debby, Bonnie. But nothing's going to hurt you. Go along, now, and don't stop any place."

"Suppose she gets lost?" asked Emmy.

"How can she get lost?" Chris wanted to know. "The path doesn't fork again. All she has to do is follow her nose and keep going down."

But Emmy wasn't sure about this. In spite of

the red toboggan cap like Debby's, Bonnie looked to Emmy like the same small sister.

"You go that way, Bonnie, and I'll go this, and I'll beat you to the Wattersons'," said Debby, who was tired of waiting. "You can run if you want to, and I'll still beat you."

That decided the matter. Bonnie started off in a trot along the top of the mountain. Debby began hurriedly walking down the mountain by the roundabout way. Chris followed Debby, and Emmy followed Chris. Emmy kept looking back as long as she could see a sign of a red toboggan cap moving along the top of the mountain.

In half an hour Debby and Chris and Emmy came walking up to the Wattersons' gate. Out of the front door of the house burst Andy. Out of the door after him rushed a little black puppy, biting at his shoestrings.

"Look! Look at the puppy!" shouted Debby. She stooped and stroked the puppy's back.

"What's his name, Andy?" asked Chris.

"Tiger," said Andy.

"Here, Tige! Here, Tige!" called Chris. He began running in circles, with Tiger cutting capers at his heels.

"He doesn't look much like a tiger," said Emmy. "He doesn't look one bit fierce."

"He can bark real fierce," said Chris. "Real tigerish."

"He looks like nothing but a little puppy to me," said Emmy, stooping to smooth back the

soft, floppy ears. "He looks like the sort of puppy that climbs out of one scrape right into another. All the way up to his ears."

Three Watterson children smaller than Andy came running out of the house. They began to play with the puppy too. They were as noisy as seven children and one puppy always are.

"Is Bonnie here, Andy?" asked Emmy, when she could make herself heard.

"Bonnie? No," said Andy.

"Then I beat her," said Debby.

Father and Mr. Watterson came along just then with a load of wood on the wagon. They began unloading the wood in the woodlot.

"Didn't Bonnie come with you?" asked Father, when he saw Debby, Chris and Emmy.

They told Father what had happened on top of the mountain. Father said nothing, but, as he unloaded the wood, he kept watching the steep path for a sign of Bonnie.

"How long ago did you leave her?" Father asked after a while.

"Long enough for her to be here," said Emmy.

"She was wearing her new red toboggan cap," Debby told him. "She felt as big as Althy, wearing it. She felt as big as the schoolteacher."

Again Father looked up the mountain path for Bonnie. Mr. Watterson looked too. Chris and Emmy and Debby looked, and Andy, and the other three Wattersons. Even Tiger looked. As far as they could see, there was no sign of a little white-haired, blue-eyed girl wearing a red toboggan cap.

Andy and Chris began to play with Tiger again.

Suddenly Father cupped his hand to his ear.

"Be quiet, boys," he said. "I heard something."

"Sounded like Bonnie, didn't it?" asked Mr. Watterson.

"Be quiet, Tige!" scolded Andy.

All of them stood still and listened — Father and Mr. Watterson, Chris and Andy, Emmy and Debby, and the three little Wattersons. Tiger stood the stillest of all.

In a minute the sound came again. It came faintly from a distance, but this time there was no doubt about it. It was Bonnie, crying a frightened cry.

Tiger arched his small back and growled.

"Wonder what happened to her?" said Chris. "She's screaming at the top of her lungs."

"She's saying something," Father said. "Can any of you make out what she's saying?"

They listened again. No one could tell what Bonnie was saying, but they could tell from the the sound of her crying that she was growing more frightened every minute.

"I shouldn't have let her go alone," said Emmy. Tears stood in Emmy's eyes. Goose bumps broke out on her arms.

"She can't be lost," said Chris.

"The path is as plain as the nose on her face," said Andy.

"Maybe she fell down and hurt herself," said Debby. "I fell down one time on that path when I was no bigger than Bonnie, and hurt myself."

"You can tell she isn't hurt," said Mr. Watterson. "If you listen, you can tell she's running back and forth."

Father started climbing out of the wagon. "I'll run up the mountain and see what's happened to her," he said.

"Maybe she's seen a wild animal — a 'possum or a skunk," said Mr. Watterson.

Mr. Watterson, too, climbed out of the wagon, and ran into the house. "Hold the horses, Andy," he called back. "You and Chris."

In a minute he came out of the house, carrying a rifle on his shoulder. "I'll take this along in case we need it," he said. He hurried up the steep mountain path behind Father, the rifle on his shoulder.

Chris and Andy held the horses to keep them from running away with the wagon. Emmy and Debby, the three little Wattersons and Tiger stood quietly, their eyes fastened on the mountain path. Up on the mountain Bonnie's crying grew more and more frightened.

"I wish I hadn't let her go alone," whispered Emmy.

Debby stood close to Emmy. "Do you suppose she's seen a bear?" Debby asked.

"Nobody has seen a bear on that mountain for years," Andy said. "And besides," he added, "the bears have gone to bed for the winter now."

Up the steep mountain path climbed Father as fast as he could go. Behind him climbed Mr. Watterson, his rifle on his shoulder.

When Father reached the top of the mountain, he caught sight of Bonnie through the bare trees. She was running to and fro on the path, crying so loudly that all the little beasts and birds that live on a mountain — blue jays and cardinals, squirrels and chipmunks — had hidden deep in the woods.

"Bonnie!" called Father. "What's the matter, Bonnie?"

But Bonnie could not hear him above her crying.

"No telling what's happened to make a child scream like that," said Mr. Watterson. He took his rifle from his shoulder and held it ready to shoot in case he saw a wild animal.

"Bonnie!" shouted Father again.

When Bonnie turned and saw Father, she ran to him. Her eyes were red, and her face was

streaked from crying. Her white hair was tousled, and one copper-toed shoe was untied. In one hand she gripped a handful of feathery green moss.

Father stooped and put his arms around her. "What's the matter, honey?" he asked.

"I — I lost my — toboggan cap!" cried Bonnie. "I can't — can't find it anywhere!"

"You lost your toboggan!" said Father. He smiled to himself as he wiped the tears from Bonnie's face. "Isn't that a little thing to make such a big noise about?" he asked.

Mr. Watterson smiled, too, and shouldered his rifle.

"It was — my new toboggan," sobbed Bonnie. "Like Debby's."

"Where did you lose it?" asked Father.

"I don't know," cried Bonnie. "I was gathering moss — for Debby's playhouse, and I — and I felt on my head for my toboggan, and it — it was gone."

"Let's walk back along the path and see if we can find it," suggested Father.

"I'll go back down the mountain and tell the others," said Mr. Watterson.

Hand in hand, Father and Bonnie walked back along the path toward the fork where one path branched off and led by a roundabout way down to the valley. Before they reached the fork, they spied something red dangling from a low limb that branched over the path.

"Wonder what that is?" asked Father.

"My toboggan cap," said Bonnie, in a small voice. She no longer felt as big as Debby. She scarcely felt as big as Bonnie.

"Looks like that limb was playing tag with you," said Father. "When you walked underneath, it swayed down and took your toboggan off without your knowing it."

Bonnie said nothing at all. She was thinking about Debby. Whenever Debby played tag, she never gave up until she got the last tag. That was the way all six-year-old girls played tag. It would take more than a new red toboggan cap with a white tassel to make her as big as Debby, she guessed.

Father took the red toboggan from the limb, being careful not to pull a thread. He smoothed Bonnie's tangled white hair back from her forehead, wiped her eyes once more, and pulled the toboggan on her head.

"Now!" he said. "You look as good as new!"

That made Bonnie feel almost as big as herself again.

"Suppose you ride on my back," said Father. He turned his back and Bonnie climbed on.

Away down the path they hurried, in the direction of the Wattersons' house.

"Watch out for your toboggan," said Father. "Don't let another limb get your tag."

They came to the tree where Bonnie had been gathering a moss carpet for Debby's playhouse.

"I don't believe you have enough moss to carpet Debby's playhouse, have you?" asked Father, looking at the small strip of moss squeezed in Bonnie's hand. "Suppose we take time to gather some more. I believe we could carry enough to carpet a playhouse for you too. Don't you think so?"

Bonnie climbed down from Father's back.

"If I walked, we could," she said. "We could fill your hands with moss, and mine too. I don't need to ride on your back," she said. "I'm not so little."

The Journey

THE NEXT week Father saddled Mag one morning at sunup and rode off across the river. He had business to attend to in the town across the eastern mountains, and he wouldn't be home until Saturday.

When he came riding home at sundown on Saturday, he had in his saddlebags presents for everyone — for Mother, for Althy and Chris, for Emmy and Debby and Bonnie.

To Mother, he brought a new comb to wear in her dark brown hair — a comb of golden brown, made of the shell of a tortoise, and shaped like a beautiful old lace fan. At once Mother put the comb in her hair. She looked like the picture of the princess in Emmy's third reader.

To Althy, Father brought a string of beads the color of the pink altheas that bloomed by the front gate during the summertime. Althy

fastened the beads around her neck at once, and
went to look at herself in the mirror. She held
the beads against the bow of pink ribbon tied
at the bottom of her light brown hair, and
noticed that they were exactly the same color.

"I'll wear the beads tomorrow," she said. "I
want to show them to Margy Sawyer."

To Chris, Father brought a pencil box with
pictures of cowboys on the front of it. In it
were six long, slick, yellow, brand-new pencils.
The minute Chris saw them he whistled a long,

loud whistle. Then he took his knife from his pocket and began sharpening the pencils.

"I'm going to take them to school on Monday," he said, "all of them, and show them to Andy Watterson. Look! They've got erasers."

To Emmy, Father brought a story book. Right away Emmy sprawled on the floor, opened the book, and began to read on page one.

To Debby, Father brought a pair of ice skates with thin, shining blades, and straps for fastening the skates to her shoes.

"Oh!" cried Debby. "How can I wait until January? I wish the river would freeze tonight!"

She fastened the skates on her shoes and balanced herself on the bright rag carpet on the living-room floor.

To Bonnie, Father brought a handkerchief. It was just her size, and in one corner of it there was a picture of Little Red Riding Hood going to see her grandmother.

Bonnie spread the handkerchief on a chair

and looked at Red Riding Hood a long time. Then she folded it neatly.

"I'm going to save it for a journey," she said.

"A journey!" laughed Chris. "Where are you going?"

"A journey!" laughed Debby. "You're not going anywhere, honey."

Bonnie went quietly up the stairs and laid the handkerchief away neatly in a little box that contained all her treasures — one piece of blue glass that had been melted in the fire, two glossy brown buckeyes with a round white eye in the top of each one, the arrowheads Chris and Emmy and Debby had given her, and one blue jay's feather.

From that day on, Bonnie wondered about the journey — where she would go, and when she should go, and what she should do when she got there. Every morning she left her play, went up the stairs, opened her treasure box and touched the handkerchief. Then she put the lid

on the box again, went back to her play, and waited.

One morning in December Chris and Althy, Emmy and Debby were getting ready to go to school. A cold wind was howling in the mountain passes, warning the children to wear their mittens and to bundle up snugly.

"Bonnie," said Father, "how would you like to go to school today?"

"Oh, do let her!" begged Emmy.

"She can sit with me part of the time," said Althy, "and look at pictures."

"She can recite my lessons with me," said Debby. "Maybe she can learn to read."

"When Bonnie can read," said Mother, "she has finished being a little girl and has started being big. But you must get ready quickly, Bonnie, if you are going to school. The children can't wait for you. They mustn't be late."

"Shall I wear my new red toboggan cap, Mother?" asked Bonnie.

"Yes," said Mother. "Come, let me scrub your neck and ears. Children have to be extra clean when they go to school."

In the kitchen Mother scrubbed away on Bonnie's neck and ears, giving orders all the while. "Althy, run get Bonnie's Sunday dress. Chris, give her shoes a little shining. Emmy, bring clean stockings for her. Debby, brush her coat off. Here, Father, hand me the comb and brush. We'll have her ready in a jiffy."

Exactly in a jiffy Bonnie was ready. Out the door they started to school, Althy and Chris, Emmy and Debby, and Bonnie, holding tightly to Father's hand.

At the gate Bonnie stopped.

"Wait a minute," she said. "I forgot something."

Into the house and up the stairs she ran. Straight to the treasure box she hurried, opened the lid, and took out the handkerchief with

Little Red Riding Hood in the corner. Then down the stairs she ran again, and out to the gate.

"Why, Bonnie!" cried Debby. "What are you doing with your handkerchief? I thought you were saving it for a journey!"

"This is a journey," said Bonnie.

"School?" asked Chris. "Do you think school's a journey?"

Emmy stooped and kissed Bonnie. "School isn't a journey, honey," she laughed.

"We go to school every day, sugar," Debby told her.

"But I don't go to school every day," said Bonnie. "This is the first time I have been to school."

For a moment Bonnie was puzzled. She wondered what made a journey. She was soaped and scrubbed. She was polished, and brushed, and buttoned into her Sunday dress. She had her new red toboggan cap on her head. She was going to a place where she had never been in her life. And when she got there, she was going to finish being little. Surely, all those things added together made a journey, she thought.

"School is a journey, isn't it Father?" she asked.

"Indeed it is," said Father. "School is the most splendid journey a child can take. Hold tight to Red Riding Hood now, and we'll be off."

They turned to wave good-by to Mother

Then, hand in hand, Bonnie and Father followed the others down the road.

At the crossroads the four Sawyers were waiting for them. The Sawyers waited every morning at the crossroads, in all kinds of weather.

Off they trooped down the road together, the four Sawyers, Althy and Chris, Emmy and Debby, Father, and Bonnie, carrying her handkerchief with Red Riding Hood in the corner. They were noisy now, all but Bonnie, who was

wondering how it felt to finish forever being little.

When they rounded the bend in the road, they saw the three Huffs waiting for them. The three Huffs waited at the bend in the road every morning, in all kinds of weather.

Down the road toward the footbridge they went, the three Huffs, the four Sawyers, Althy and Chris, Emmy and Debby, Father, and Bonnie, carrying her handkerchief with Red Riding Hood in the corner. They were noisier than ever now, all but Bonnie, who was wondering how it felt to be big enough to write on a blackboard with a long white piece of chalk.

At the footbridge the five Wattersons were waiting for them. The Wattersons waited at the footbridge every morning, in all kinds of weather. Together they made so much noise, the five Wattersons, the three Huffs, the four Sawyers, Althy and Chris, Emmy and Debby, that Bonnie could not tell what she was wondering about.

The footbridge was high above the river. Each end of it was fastened to the trunk of a tree, so that it swung like a hammock. From each end of the bridge to the ground was built a ramp of saplings.

Holding Father's hand, Bonnie started up the ramp to the bridge. When she looked down through the cracks between the saplings, she could see the earth and fallen leaves and bushes. Underneath her the tops of young trees, which grew on the river bank, waved in the wind. It frightened her to look down into the tops of trees. And what a long time it took her to climb to the bridge!

"You'll never get to the bridge, Bonnie," said Debby, "stepping on every sapling in the ramp. Why do you crawl along like a snail?"

Bonnie glanced up. Nobody else, she noticed, was climbing the ramp like a snail crawling. Chris and Andy pretended they wore seven-league boots, and they reached the bridge in

five giant strides, whistling as they climbed. Margy Sawyer and Althy were so busy talking that they didn't look where they were going. Even Debby, although she had to look sharply where she was going, walked along without holding to anyone.

The bridge was more frightening than the ramp. With so many people on it, it swung and bounced and swayed, until Bonnie began to feel that a journey was quite a dangerous thing.

The others didn't seem to think the bridge

dangerous. Chris ran across it, with Andy Watterson at his heels. Margy Sawyer and Althy walked across without holding to the cables stretched beside the bridge. Even Debby, although she held to the cables, looked down and yoo-hooed to the fish in the river, while Emmy leaned over the cable on one side to drop a paper boat into the water, then over the cable on the other side to watch it sail under the bridge and bob along on the ripples.

The most frightening thing of all was the downhill ramp on the other bank of the river. Bonnie stepped off the bridge onto the first sapling. The ramp was so steep she felt she would surely topple headlong to the ground.

"Come on, Bonnie!" called Debby. "Walk down like this."

Debby ran down the ramp as if it were the hill back of the stable. But Bonnie couldn't run. When she looked through the cracks between the saplings and saw the treetops waving, she was almost too frightened to move. She had to plod along, one sapling at a time, holding tightly to Father's hand.

She was still frightened when she reached the foot of the ramp, for she had begun to think of the journey back home in the evening when she would have to go up and down the ramps and cross the bridge again. A journey wasn't much fun, she thought to herself, if she had to be frightened all the time.

Right away Bonnie began to wonder how she might cross the bridge and go up and down the ramps in the evening without at all being frightened.

She wondered about it the rest of the way

to the schoolhouse. She wondered about it as Father said good-by to them at the schoolhouse door.

"I'll come by when school is out," said Father. "Have a fine journey, Bonnie."

She wondered about it as she sat between Althy and Margy Sawyer, and looked at the strange pictures in Althy's geography, and drew on a sheet of paper with Margy's colored crayons.

She wondered about it at recess time when the children played chicky-ma-chicky-ma-craney-crow, and Chris, who was the mother hen, drove Andy Watterson, who was the witch, away from Bonnie because she was a baby chicken and very young and tender.

She wondered about it at noon when she ate her lunch with Emmy. She wondered about it when she went to the front of the room with Debby to recite Debby's lesson.

Bonnie sat close to Debby and looked on her book. It had many colored pictures and many strange words that Debby could read right off.

"I see a squirrel," read Debby. "The squirrel is in a tree. Watch him jump."

Clarissy Huff could read too. So could Janie Sawyer. They knew almost all the words. Maybe that was why they could cross the bridge and go up and down the ramps so easily, thought Bonnie, because they knew the words in their books.

Bonnie sat watching Debby. Debby held up her hand whenever she wanted to ask a question. Bonnie held up her hand too.

"Yes, Bonnie," said the teacher. "What is it?"

"Please, may I learn *cat?*" asked Bonnie.

"Certainly you may," said the teacher. "We'll all help you, won't we, girls?"

They turned back to the first page in the book and found *cat*. The teacher wrote *cat* on on the board. Janie found *cat* on a card on the teacher's desk. Clarissy turned to a page that had *cat* on it three times, and helped Bonnie to find them, all three of them.

"Wouldn't you like to write *cat* on the blackboard until time to go home?" asked the teacher. "It won't be long now."

So Bonnie took a long white piece of chalk and wrote *cat* on the blackboard. It didn't look exactly like the teacher's *cat*. Even when Debby held her hand and helped her write, it didn't look quite like the teacher's. But Debby said it was much better than she could write when she was four.

Just then school was over, and Father came by. Down the road they went toward the footbridge, the five Wattersons, the three Huffs, the four Sawyers, Althy and Chris, Emmy and Debby, and behind them all, hand in hand, Father and Bonnie.

Up the ramp they went, Chris and Andy whistling as they pretended they wore seven-league boots, Althy and Margy Sawyer chattering away without looking where they were going, Debby singing as she walked ahead of Bonnie.

Bonnie, with her eyes on Debby, put her foot on the first sapling. Before she knew it, she skipped two saplings, and then three, just as Debby was doing. She let go of Father's hand.

"Better hold on," Father cautioned her.

"I don't need to," said Bonnie. "Not any more. I can read now. I can read *cat*."

"Oh, ho!" laughed Father. "So you don't need to hold on because you can read *cat!*"

"I don't need to hold your hand crossing the bridge, either," Bonnie said.

"Well, now, how does that happen?" asked

Father. "Have you grown into such a big girl in one day?"

"Yes," she told him. "When you can read *cat*, you've finished being little forever and ever."

On the bridge Bonnie held tightly to the cables. When Debby yoo-hooed to the fish, she yoo-hooed too, though not very loudly. Once she glanced down at Emmy's paper boat bobbing along on the ripples.

At the downhill ramp, which was the most frightening of all, Bonnie walked behind Debby and didn't hold Father's hand. She couldn't go down so fast as Debby. She had to step on every sapling. But she went down alone, without holding to anything at all.

At the footbridge the Wattersons left them. At the bend in the road the Huffs turned west. At the crossroads the Sawyers said good-by until tomorrow.

When they were almost home, Bonnie stooped to pick up something she spied half-buried beside the road.

"Look what I found!" she cried. "Look, everybody!"

"An arrowhead!" said Father. "Your first one!"

Althy and Chris, Emmy and Debby crowded around her to examine the arrowhead. It was small, chipped of dark gray flint.

"It's nothing unusual," said Chris. "It's the most ordinary kind."

114

"But that's the hardest kind to see," said Debby.

"I'll help you hunt a box to put your collection in when we get home," said Emmy. "You'll probably find one every day or so now."

Mother was waiting for them at the door.

"Did you have a nice journey, Bonnie?" asked Mother.

"Yes, Mother," said Bonnie. But she didn't tell Mother she had finished being little and started being big. That, she was sure, everyone could see at a glance.

"I learned to read," she said.

"And she found an arrowhead," said Debby. "Her very first one."

"What will you do with your handkerchief, now that you've taken it on a journey?" asked Mother.

Bonnie looked down at the handkerchief. It was squeezed into a ball from being held so tightly in dangerous places, and poor Little Red

Riding Hood was mussed so badly that not even the wolf, not even her own grandmother, would have recognized her.

Bonnie smoothed the wrinkles out of the handkerchief.

"I'll just keep it," she said, "to remember when I was little."